THE
WATER MAIDEN
OF LEALOS

CALLENLAS CHRONICLES

THE
WATER MAIDEN
OF LEALOS

H. R. HESS

Reformation
Lightning

Reformation Lightning

www.ReformationLightning.com

First published by Reformation Lightning in 2023

Cover design by JT Branding (www.jtbranding.com)
Typeset by Pete Barnsley (CreativeHoot.com)

Printed and bound in Great Britain

ISBN 978-1-916669-02-4

Reformation Lightning, an imprint of 10Publishing
Unit C, Tomlinson Road, Leyland, PR25 2DY, England

Email: info@10ofthose.com
Website: www.10ofthose.com

1 3 5 7 10 8 6 4 2

To Bethan,

without whom these books
would never have made it into print.
Thank you.

MAP FROM RUNA'S TIME

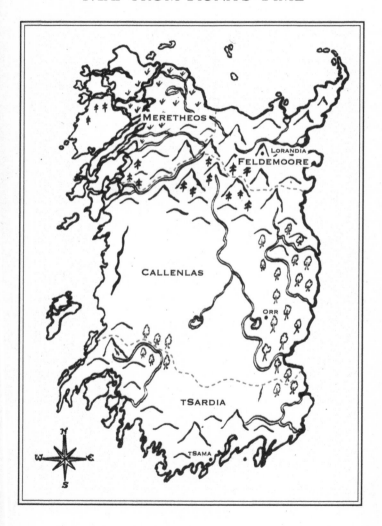

MAP FROM ELEOS'S TIME

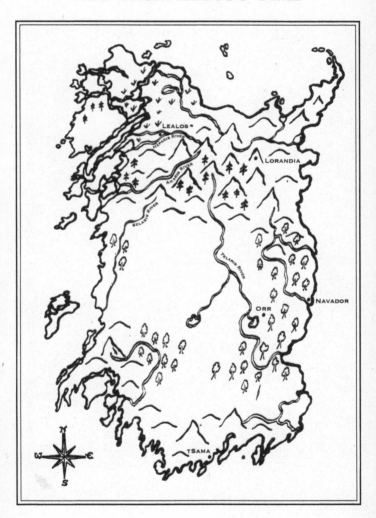

CHAPTER 1

Runa.

The voice broke like a wave into her consciousness, drawing her from a deep sleep.

Runa, I'm sorry to wake you.

Usually alert even when sleeping in her own bedchamber in Feldemoore, Runa groaned and turned over. She had been working with newly sworn skyriders all day, running from dragon to dragon to fend off disaster, or at least the loss of an arm. Only one rider had come away with singed hair and Runa was counting it a successful day. But she was exhausted.

I must speak with you.

Runa dragged her attention to the Sender.

It's still dark, she managed to Send, then realised it was King Elior, and sat up in bed. *My King!*

Runa could feel his presence shimmering like light on water and, despite the miles between them, she sensed the warmth in his voice. Unlike most distant Sendings, his were crystal clear, like the light of the stars on a cloudless winter night.

I assume it's urgent, Runa Sent. She had worked hard on mind arts in her training, but still struggled. It was the King who covered the miles of land and sea that lay between them.

I am afraid so. You heard, I presume, of the death of the King of tSardia?

Runa, still fighting sleep, forced her sluggish brain to focus. Yes, she had heard of the sudden death of King Lakesh, several months ago now. His daughter had become Queen of tSardia at only twenty-three.

Queen Junal has been quite militant in declaring her right to the throne of Callenlas. My Ambassador in tSama has met with the Queen, but while she professes to want friendship, I believe she is intent on war. The King's anger flickered orange in his Sending. *We have worked so hard to keep the peace between our lands. I will not allow another conflict to trouble my people in Callenlas.*

Ten years had passed since Runa and Zaphreth got caught up in the most recent conflict between tSardia and Callenlas. How could the peace crumble already, when lives had been given to establish it?

What can I do, my King? she asked. As a skyrider, her main task now was to help train other novice riders. Perhaps the King wanted her to step up the training programme and involve more recruits or return to Orr to work with the novice skyriders there.

I want you to go to Orr, and speak to my Master of Histories, Elior replied.

History? Runa could not hide her dismay.

I do not have time to explain now. You must trust me, Runa, as your King and as your friend. Master Horgin will meet you tomorrow, in the library at Orr.

Runa twisted her mouth, hesitant.

My King, you know history is ... Runa searched for a diplomatic way to say, boring, dull, awful. *... not my best subject.*

The King's amusement did not help Runa.

Trust me, was all he said. His laughter quickly died. *I know I need not impress upon you how important it is that we prevent this war.*

Runa's stomach clenched, and a shadow fell over her mind.

I know, she replied.

May the light of the stars guide you, Runa.

I hear and obey, my King.

CHAPTER 2

In the gathering dusk, Runa steered Shari slightly east, towards the glimmering lights of Orr. She had been unable to leave her duties in Lorandia at short notice and had spent most of the day with her novice riders before flying south. Now, she was tired, and longing for bed. She could see the torches on the ground to guide riders to the landing field, just outside the city walls.

Shari touched down nimbly, shaking her wings and head before crouching so Runa could slip off. She left Shari in the capable hands of one of the dragon-tenders, then jogged to the narrow gate; a city entrance reserved for riders. To her irritation, she found the door locked. She rapped on the wood.

"Open up," she called.

"Who seeks admittance?" asked a voice from the other side of the door.

"Runa, Skyrider of Feldemoore," Runa sighed. "You knew I was coming!"

She heard the sound of the bolts being drawn, but as she tapped her foot, two more dragons swept down onto the landing field, one a blue like Shari, the other a formidable black. In the distance, against the setting Day-Star, she could see the silhouette of a third flying towards the city.

"What's going on?" she asked as the door creaked open. She recognised the guard, a new recruit to the King's service. "You shouldn't lock the door until dark."

"Extra security measures, my Lady," the guard said, bobbing a funny, brisk bow. He was wearing full battle gear: an oversized helmet that sat just above his eyeline, a breastplate over a chain-mail shirt, and a large spear that kept getting in the way as Runa tried to squeeze past in the narrow passage.

"What for?"

But the guard's gaze fell on the two riders now approaching the door behind Runa. "Who seeks admittance?" he demanded again, his voice quivering.

Mystified, Runa made her way along the stone passage. It ran beneath the city, leading directly to the palace itself, so that skyriders could quickly come and go. There was no room to keep dragons inside the city itself, with its narrow streets and crowded housing.

Emerging into the lower rooms of the palace, Runa intended to head for the library to find the Master of Histories. She quickly perceived that there was more afoot than extra security measures. The palace was busy. In the lower rooms, servants and novices scurried about, carrying armfuls of folded standards, stacks of spears, and baskets of provisions. As Runa climbed to the higher rooms, she found an unusual number of riders standing about, talking in serious voices, looking over lists, and giving instructions to eager-faced novices.

A sense of foreboding crept into Runa's belly, like a slowly wakening worm. She knew only too well what preparations for military action looked like.

Across the room she spotted Kels, one of the skyriders who had trained with her.

"Runa," he grinned, offering her his palm, which she met distractedly with her own.

"Why is everyone preparing for battle?" she asked quietly.

"tSardia," he whispered back, grin fading. "We heard today that they've moved forces towards the border."

Runa's stomach-worm woke fully, baring sharp teeth.

"I thought the Queen sought a peaceful solution?" she said.

Kels shrugged.

"That's what tSardia claims." His voice was bleak. "But the troops are there."

Runa pressed her lips together and fought to keep her breathing calm. Since becoming a skyrider, she had been involved in a few small skirmishes with pirates in the south, and flesh-traders in Feldemoore. War was another thing entirely. Runa fought to keep the vivid memories of the last war from filling her head. The scrape of metal against bone. The screams of young men pierced with arrows or blades. The rows of dead, laid out after the battle.

Runa stepped back from Kels and the group of riders. She moved to the window and drew in a gulp of air, trying to steady herself against the stone ledge. Through the glass, she could see the plains of Callenlas stretching south-west, pastureland, fields, and then, beyond her sight, the tSardian desert. Was it really only ten years since she had hidden with Zaphreth, while Elior battled the dark star, Lur?

Glancing back at the busy room, she could see riders-in-training waiting to be sent on errands, while newly qualified riders hung about in nervous clusters. They looked so young. How many would return, should war break out?

A surge of anger flared inside Runa. This war had to be stopped.

CHAPTER 3

Tiredness forgotten, Runa jogged through the palace rooms to the library. Master Horgin was waiting for her there, his grey head bent over an alarming stack of books and papers. She hoped he did not expect her to read it all.

"Good evening, Master Horgin," she said.

The Master of Histories jumped, looking around like a startled rabbit.

"Ah, the Princess Runa, I presume?"

Runa smiled. She had met the Master at a couple of formal banquets at Orr, and he never once remembered. His rather vague expression was underpinned by permanently unfocused blue eyes, as if his attention was fixed upon the thoughts in his head.

"Just 'Runa' is fine," she replied, greeting him palm to palm.

"Please, sit," he said.

Runa settled on a wooden bench at the table, while Master Horgin sat back down in his carved chair.

"I have to be honest," Runa said, "I'm struggling to see how history can help with tSardia."

Horgin's mouth fell open in horror, and Runa immediately regretted her words.

"History is everything!" the Master exclaimed. "Why, why ... if we do not know where we have come from, how can we possibly know where we are going?"

Runa nodded politely, still unconvinced.

"King Elior has asked us to look into the division of Callenlas," Horgin explained. "A very turbulent time. You know, of course, that the Princes were established to rule Callenlas in Elior's place when he left to take the light of the stars to other lands. Well, after two hundred years or so, the Princes began to title themselves 'Kings' and viewed Elior as more of a legend than as the true King of Callenlas.

"Prince Arten came to the throne in the three-hundred-and-ninety-first year of the stars; he called himself King Arten, and his wife the Queen. They had four sons."

"I remember this," Runa said, her history lessons flooding back to her mind from years ago. The story had always struck her as sad. "Arten died young – a hunting accident, I think? tSardin was the eldest, and thought he had a right to inherit the throne, but Ilfian claimed his father wanted him to be Prince, or King."

"Almost," Horgin nodded encouragingly, beaming at Runa. "The Kings had fallen into a habit of leaving the throne to their eldest sons, as was the custom of most nations. But in the case of Callenlas, by law it was not meant to be so. The next Prince was meant to be appointed by the consensus of the five Guardians and the existing Prince, and by Elior's assent. However, by Arten's day this had mostly been forgotten.

"And so, yes, when he died young, Prince tSardin thought the throne was his birthright, as the eldest. Some of the King's council, however, including the Guardian of Orr, claimed that King Arten had left his throne to Ilfian, his second son."

"Why would they think that?"

"Supposedly, King Arten wrote it in a will on his deathbed, but tSardin's supporters denied it."

"So, this led to war."

"Indeed."

"Well, there we are then," Runa grinned, her eyes alight. "We just have to find the will, and that will put an end to tSardia's complaint – they'd have no claim to the throne of Callenlas; in fact," she continued, growing in excitement, "it would mean that tSardia shouldn't exist at all!"

Horgin gave a sad sort of smile.

"Many history Masters have dedicated years to finding the document," he said. "Most have concluded that either it never existed, or that it was destroyed."

"Oh."

"But …" Master Horgin glanced around like a nervous hamster, in case, Runa supposed, any tSardian spies might be hiding in the library. Horgin leaned forward and whispered with a startling intensity, "I have been wondering whether tSardia might secretly possess the document in their records!"

He leaned back, and since he clearly expected Runa to be impressed, she nodded and widened her eyes.

"Well," Horgin modified himself with a tilt of his head, "at least tSardia might own other letters or diaries so far unseen by our Masters, that might prove whether it existed or give us an idea of what happened to it. Most of the Masters of History have agreed that one of Ilfian's closest advisors was working against him, in support of tSardin. They may have stolen or even destroyed Arten's will ... if, of course, it even existed."

Of course, Runa thought, there would certainly be official annals and letters in the tSardian records, perhaps even personal ones. Somewhere in tSardia, there had to be something that would provide a clue about who had been helping tSardin against Ilfian. But surely, they wouldn't allow anyone to go rooting around in their official records?

Even as she thought it, a horrible suspicion began to creep into Runa's mind.

"I suggested to the King that someone might request access to the tSardian historical records, and he recommended you."

Runa sighed.

"Look," she said, "I'm not a historian. If you asked me to lead a fleet of skyriders over the border, or even to the battle, I would. But with this, I won't have the first clue what I'm looking for."

"Just … just read this." The Master fished through his papers, and pressed a slim, kid-bound book into Runa's hands.

"What is it?"

"It is the diary of Eleos," Horgin said. "She was the daughter of the Marsh-Reif, ruler of the Western Marshes, sent to Orr to study with the Princes of Callenlas when they were all young, before the division was even thought of. She married tSardin, becoming the first Queen of tSardia after the war."

Runa flicked the book to find a beautiful script filling each page.

"Do be careful with it," Master Horgin pleaded. "It's two hundred and fifty years old."

Runa sighed again. History and now reading. Was King Elior trying to test her loyalty?

"Now, I must go to bed," Master Horgin stood decisively. "I'm not as young as I once was. In the morning we can make arrangements for your journey to tSama. In fact, the Ambassador Rellian of Feldemoore is already expecting you."

Runa opened her mouth to object to the Master's plan, but he had already blown out the lamp and was shuffling towards the door, leaving her in darkness.

CHAPTER 4

Runa sat in the bed of the small guest room she had been given for the night, high in one of the towers of the palace. It was late, nearly midnight, but she could still hear activity in the rooms all around her, preparations for defence continuing even after the Day-Star had set. Runa had begun to appreciate why the history of the division might be important; but why had Elior chosen her, of all his riders, for this mission? She was no historian, and no reader, either. Even the narrow diary Master Horgin had given her filled her with dread.

Runa opened the soft, leather cover and ran her fingers over the neatly hand-written pages.

Well, here I am, began Eleos's first entry. *The great capital of Orr.*

The journey from the Marshlands was long, and it seemed to rain every day, though I'm sure that's not quite true. The first part wasn't too bad, travelling on the barges and waterways of the Marshes, but once we left the boats it was all on horseback, and sleeping in tents, and quite uncomfortable.

I realise most people would love to be educated in a palace, but I am not used to these luxurious surroundings. I am a Water Maiden of Lealos, the daughter of the Marsh-Reif, not a Princess. I feel out of place and stupid. Even the clothes Mama and I sewed, and thought were so fine, are plain compared to the jewels and silks of the King and Queen.

They call themselves King Arten and Queen Olenda, though at home we still term them Prince and Princess. They have forgotten, I think, that Elior is King, and this makes me feel less at home than ever.

I know Papa hopes I will marry one of the King's sons. The alliance would be good for the Marshlands. But I do not think I am suited to this role. I am not clever, I am not quick with words, I am not beautiful. I do not think I would make a good wife to a Prince, or even a Governor.

But Papa only sees what he wants to see. He thinks I will learn and grow ... and perhaps I will. But I already miss our beautiful waterways, and how the Heparis shines in the Day-Star.

Ilfian – the only one of the Princes who has shown me any real kind of welcome – tells me there is a lake nearby, an hour's ride from the palace. Perhaps we can go tomorrow and take a skiff out onto the water. Perhaps then I will feel less homesick.

Runa felt a flicker of pity for this girl, sent so far from her home to a strange world, bound by duty and her father's will. She had felt a similar sense of entrapment all those years ago, so much so that she had run away from her father and the restrictions of royal life.

She turned the page.

I completed my first week of lessons today. The King and Queen have appointed tutors to oversee their sons' education. As I feared, I am sadly behind the others.

'The others' are the four royal Princes, and two other children from noble families of Callenlas. tSardin, the oldest Prince, is King Arten's heir. He is handsome, clever, very good at sword-fighting and horse-riding but, unfortunately, he knows it. His hair and eyes are very dark, but rather dazzling all the same. I can see how he would make a good King. But I am still troubled by how King Elior seems forgotten by everyone.

Ilfian, the second son, is fourteen, so only a year older than me (tSardin is fifteen). Ilfian has even darker hair than tSardin, but his eyes are grey like the waters of Lealos. I watched the boys in their sword lessons this afternoon, and Ilfian is good, perhaps even better than tSardin ... but he lacks tSardin's ruthlessness, and so he is beaten every time. His brother delights in it, and I think it hurts Ilfian's feelings, though he tries to hide it. He is gentler than tSardin; and one of the only people here who talks freely of Elior.

Felden comes next; he's twelve, and looks more like his mother, the Queen, with soft brown hair and amber eyes. He likes to push himself forward and tries to compete with his brothers in everything. I don't blame him, growing up with two clever, athletic older brothers must be difficult.

Erchen is only ten, and always seems to be left behind. Ilfian tries to help him, but tSardin enjoys being the best, and does not see how Erchen feels left out.

Thankfully, I am not the only girl among four boys. The Prince – I mean King Arten – and the Queen have also taken in a few others to learn with their sons.

Lady Istria (she insists on being called 'Lady') is the daughter of the Governor of tSama, the foremost city of the south. She is very beautiful, with long, dark hair, very clever and wears such elegant clothes. She barely speaks to me, and most of the time I am glad, because I seem to become tongue-tied whenever she does. But it would be nice to feel I had a friend here.

I miss home, and Mama especially.

I wonder if Morival might become my friend, in time, but she is already very close to Istria, and a little silly. She is the daughter of the Guardian of the East. Plump and pretty, with soft brown curls, and the same age as me, but she all but worships Istria.

We share a room, we three girls, but so far Istria seems to treat me more as a server, asking me to fetch things for her, and Morival follows her example. Perhaps, in time, they will grow to like me. I know I am simple, and, compared to them, from a humble home, but I do not think I am so dull as to be an unpleasant companion.

That is all of us, and I am being called to dress for dinner.

Runa paused, shifting her position on the bed to be closer to the lamplight. How difficult it must have been for a thirteen-year-old girl to be thrown into the melting pot of palace life. The next entry only confirmed her feelings.

I was going to describe the library, where we meet for lessons, but first I want to write about

Istria. I thought at first that she only looked down on me, but now I'm beginning to think she truly dislikes me.

Yesterday, we dined with King Arten and Queen Olenda. This happens twice a month unless they have official duties. It was a family dinner, and they consider it quite private, though there must have been at least ten officials present as well as the royal family, servers, and of course, us students. I can't help but contrast it with the cosy meals I used to share with Mama, Papa and Mirios. We used to sit around the fire and share simple food and tell stories or read from the histories of Callenlas.

See, now, I've blotted my writing by crying. I must stop, I really must. Papa wants me to do well here, and if I keep thinking of home I shall do very badly.

Well, this was my first banquet and I wanted to make a good impression. Mama and I had made a beautiful dress for such occasions. The silk is the colour of the waters of Lealos and shifts in the light just as the ripples do. I was so happy with it when I tried it on at home. Even Mirios said it looked nice.

I put it on and asked Morival to lace up the back for me.

"Is this your best dress?" Istria asked, frowning at me. I said yes. I did not mention that Mama and I had sewn it ourselves, as I could already sense Istria's disapproval.

"It's rather plain," Istria said.

"It's all I have."

Plain. I was right to think that the Marsh-Reif's daughter would not fit in at the great palace in Orr. My father rules the Marshes, but we are a simple people. We keep the Drogor at bay, and trade clay pots and fish with other parts of Callenlas, and we live in the wilds, in wooden houses, not stone cities. I know it is important to Papa to have the King's ear, to win his protection and help against the Drogor. I know Mirios had to stay with Papa, to learn how to be Marsh-Reif after him. If only Papa and Mama had had more children ...

I had to wear the dress, of course, but somehow Istria had stolen all the pleasure from it. I could understand her looking down on me; but why would she dislike me? She barely knows me.

But I said I would describe the library. It is already my favourite place in Orr, though perhaps after I have visited the lake, I may change my mind. We have lessons there every morning, mostly with Master Glimpsel. The doors have carved panels showing the different parts of Callenlas, and one shows Lealos, with the rivers surrounding it. The mountains rise behind it, carved so accurately in the wood that I can recognise Igris Peak and Suliel. And there is a dragon flying over the water.

And those are just the doors. Inside, it's magical. There are four arched windows, the height of the ceiling, letting in lots of light. The walls are high enough for three balconies, so that readers can access shelves of books. A spiral staircase stands at each end of the room so that you can climb up to them ... I think they must have been carved by the tree-dwellers, for they are covered in beautiful images. Ivy and climbing flowers have been carved on the central pillars of the stairs, on the bannisters, and on the upright part of each step. And little woodland creatures, carved mice and squirrels and birds, hide among the leaves. Everywhere there is something lovely to discover, and each time I go there I see something new. The whole room has a lovely, warm, secretive feeling, even though it is so large.

But I get little chance to read what I please there. I am expected to ride or dance, or sew, or take lessons on the harp, and what free time we have is often taken up with games of Cities or cards, or more riding. I do not feel I can say no when I am invited to join the others. I am here to make connections, after all, and if I hide away reading, I think Papa might be cross.

But the library is my refuge.

Runa knew the library at Orr very well. She even knew the dragon, flying on the top left panel of the grand, lea-wood doors – it had caught her eye on her first visit, several years ago. Her heart ached for Eleos, so lonely and lost, in the great palace. She knew only too well the kind of nastiness that girls like Istria could level against others.

Runa's eyes were growing heavy, and it seemed she had no choice but to embark on another long flight tomorrow. She set the diary carefully on the table beside her bed and blew out her lamp.

CHAPTER 5

Runa drew Shari in just before they reached the tSardian desert. Searching for a good landing spot, Runa took pleasure in her view of the land all around, and the pure thrill of depending on Shari to keep her from hurtling to the ground. The dragon's wings beat steadily, her large head turning at the lightest touch on her reins.

The miles of ochre sand stretched before them, shimmering in the noon light. Tilindria, the Guardian of the West, had cursed the ground between tSardia and Callenlas all those years ago when the kingdom first divided. tSardin had pushed his claim over and over, making war with Callenlas, until Tilindria created the desert as a barrier. Runa paused for a moment, remembering her own experience of war:

the clash of weapons, the screams of frightened horses, and the smells, things she usually shut from her mind. The battle must have been fought very close to here, Runa guessed. She and Zaphreth had hidden in scrub similar to that growing just south of her now. Somewhere over the border, not too far away, tSardian troops were taking up their positions. The weight of her mission pressed heavily upon her chest.

Alighting onto the dusty soil, Runa fed Shari and settled to her own lunch, giving her dragon some rest before they continued to tSama. It would be dusk before they reached the tSardian capital, right on the southern coast. The blue gulped down her meat and huffed out a blast of steam.

"Shush, Shari," Runa said, digging a sheaf of papers out of her bag. "I need to concentrate."

Before Runa left, Master Horgin had handed her a whole load of private letters between the royal family to read, as well as Eleos's diary, which Runa turned back to now. She skipped through a few entries: a visit to Lake Luriel, where Eleos finally got to paddle a boat again; a snowball fight in winter; a new tutor called Watcher Lorien. What was a Watcher? Runa wondered. One entry, about a year after Eleos arrived at Orr, caught her eye:

I think I am falling in love ... with tSardin. I know he is conceited and proud, but it is because everyone around him always gives him his way, including his parents, and all the servers and tutors. Watcher Lorien is the only one who gives him any kind of resistance, and he is clever enough to do it in such a way that tSardin cannot accuse him of insolence and have him removed from his position (which is what he has done to others in the past).

tSardin's face, his eyes ... he makes my insides tremble. And strangely, though he should consider me the lowest of us all, I am the only person he treats with any kind of regard, apart from Istria of course. I don't know why, for I am dull and far behind the others in my lessons, and still have not been able to improve my wardrobe. I am not foolish enough to imagine that tSardin would ever return my affections, but I'm certain Papa would be delighted to hear that I would now

welcome a marriage to the crown Prince – it is
exactly what he had hoped for.

Runa pursed her lips.

"Silly girl," she scoffed to Shari, who nudged Runa with her long nose. Runa reached up to scratch her dragon's blue jaw, and Shari shook her wings with pleasure. Runa repented a little of her judgement of Eleos; the girl was lonely, far from home, and did not know, after all, the devastation that tSardin would wreak upon Callenlas.

Runa skipped ahead some more.

I have had to start hiding my diary. I think Morival has been reading it with Istria and I couldn't bear it if they found out about my feelings for tSardin. They keep referring to things I've written, and then Morival giggles (she really has no subtlety). Istria gives nothing away, but I'm sure she's watching for my reaction.

I found a loose tile on my window ledge in the library. It's where I hide when I can't bear it anymore. Only I can fit on the ledge, and no one ever goes there except me – it's high, out

of sight, and very dusty (until I took a rag and
cleaned it). My diary fits perfectly in the little
gap under the tile.

Runa glanced up at the sky.

"Better go, Shari," she said. She began putting the papers from Master Horgin back into her bag, but one fluttered loose from the pages of the book. Remembering the Master's anxiety about giving her the diary, Runa snatched at it, to keep it from blowing away in the breeze. The paper was old and thin. It was a note, written in a different hand to Eleos's.

To Eos, Runa read.

Ah, Eleos, sweetest of all still waters
dancing beneath the Day-Star's light,
silken, bashful, hiding your depths,
most beautiful in the shadows of night.
Come to me now, Eos, my darling,
kiss away all my sorrow and tears,
welcome me in, your hair all in moonlight,
beside your waters I lose all my fears.

Ah, Eleos, sweetest of all still waters,
Queen of the Marshes, Queen of my heart,
under your sceptre, what care I for kingdoms,
when the Maiden of Lealos takes care of my heart.

She had found love, then, this lonely girl, in the palace at Orr. Runa pushed the note back into the pages of the diary and wondered who had written it. Would tSardin have penned something so tender? It seemed unlikely from what she knew of the Prince, though love did do strange things to people.

Looking out at the sands, Runa thought of Zaphreth, growing up near Sarreia, surrounded by desert and dust. Zaphreth had finished his training four years ago and had gone with Elior to Embassa, a land far over the eastern sea. They had Sent often at first, and written letters when couriers made the long journey over land. But Runa hadn't heard from him much lately. He was busy, she knew, with Elior's work in Embassa. Perhaps now would be a good time to reach out to him again, rekindle the friendship. He might have some insight into the history of tSardia.

Securing her bag and buttoning up her cloak, Runa swung herself onto Shari's back. The dragon launched into the air, setting out across the southern desert.

CHAPTER 6

Ambassador Rellian guided Runa through the maze of rooms and terraces that made up the palace at tSama. Runa barely noticed the expensive marble tiles as she tried to keep up, nor the ornate wall carvings, decorated with gilding and jewels. She glanced out of every window she passed, hoping in vain for a glimpse of the dragon caves. She had barely put her foot to the ground when the Ambassador of Feldemoore approached her, and Runa had been forced to leave Shari in the care of one of the tSardian dragon-keepers, rather than settling the blue herself.

Rellian wore an impeccably neat grey beard, and a long robe of red with black trim. He moved with quick, sharp movements, glancing over his shoulder all the way to Runa's room. Runa tried to be understanding, though his anxiety was making her own palms sweat and her mouth dry up. The peace between Callenlas and tSardia teetered in the balance, and somehow Elior expected her to help.

"I had hoped your visit would not be remarked upon by her majesty." Rellian spoke through lips taut with nerves. "But she has requested to meet you, and I could not refuse, of course."

"Of course." Runa's heart sank. This mission kept drawing on all her weaknesses; history, reading, and now a formal meeting as a Princess. She would have to dress nicely, and make polite small talk, when all she wanted to do was take a look at some dusty old letters and escape back to Orr as quickly as she could.

"Queen Junal has invited you to a formal banquet tomorrow evening, but she also wants to meet you privately today," Rellian added.

"Does the Queen know why I have come?" Runa asked, alarmed. Horgin had Sent to Rellian and was supposed to have stressed the secrecy of her task. She was dismayed that the Queen knew she had come at all.

Rellian glanced about himself and put his head close to Runa's to whisper.

"She has been told that you are looking for information about your ancestor, King Felden, and at the moment she has no reason to believe this has anything to do with Callenlas. As far as she knows, this is a personal interest of yours."

Runa nodded in grim acceptance. Who would have thought historical paperwork could be so fraught?

"May I suggest, my Lady, that you visit the library now, before meeting the Queen. If she works out your real motive for exploring the royal archives, she will certainly restrict your access, and it would, of course, put pressure on our own diplomatic relations ..."

Rellian cast a pleading look at Runa, who felt dizzy at the implications of her presence in tSardia. If the Queen discovered that she was working for Callenlas, it could draw her own nation of Feldemoore into the war as well.

"Which way is the library?" she asked.

"I will send a server to guide you," Rellian was apologetic. "The Queen was insistent that you do not explore the palace without a guide."

Once in the privacy of her room, Runa unpacked her small bag of belongings. The formal dress she had brought as an afterthought was sadly creased having been wadded between a spare tunic and the papers from Master Horgin. Runa shook it, and tried to smooth it out, before draping it over a chair. Hopefully the creases would fall out themselves before the formal dinner planned for the next day.

While she waited for the server, Runa leafed through the papers Master Horgin had stuffed into her hands before she left. She wanted to look at a couple while she waited for a server to show her to the library. As well as the diary, there were copies of letters, some formal, some private, from the royal family at the time of the division of the kingdom.

Runa glanced over one letter, dated four years before the death of King Arten.

Guardian Rhemos, from the palace of Orr,
To Ilfian, Prince, at the Watchtower of Navador

My dear Ilfian,
  I was told today of your departure for Navador, with Watcher Lorien. I am quite shocked at your flagrant disobedience of your

father and myself. You claim to love King Elior yet will not submit to his appointed Prince and Guardian.

Dear boy, I have lived a long life, the stars know, and I have seen many who think they are serving the King by giving up all their days in sitting, watching the sea. They have forgotten that Elior established Callenlas as a kingdom, with lands to be worked, homes to be built and kept, animals to be cared for. He wishes us to live, to love others, to work for justice and peace. It may feel very righteous to spend your days shut away, reading Elior's law and Sending to him and the other stars ... but if the law remains only on paper it is worthless. It was meant to be used, lived, put into life.

I wish you had talked with me more. I know the thought of the crown is burdensome to you, but you are young, your father is young, and it will be many years before that weight of responsibility rests upon you. Besides, your father and I hope that tSardin will change, and may still be the right Prince for Callenlas. We only wanted you to know our thoughts, and to be prepared for whatever the future may hold.

Please return to Orr, Ilfian. We will do all we can, your father and I, and the other Guardians, to help you wield what power is granted you with wisdom, justice, mercy, and love.

If you do not return, I fear what your brother will do. I fear for all of Callenlas.

Rhemos

Runa raised her eyebrows. So, Arten had spoken to both Ilfian and tSardin about inheriting the throne years before it happened. Questions filled her mind. Who *was* this Watcher Lorien, and why had Ilfian left Orr with him? Was that what Rhemos meant by disobedience?

And why had Ilfian been so resistant to becoming King? Runa's experience told her that everyone wanted power; everyone imagined that they would make a good ruler, not realising – as she did, from watching her father – how unimaginably difficult and demanding it could be.

Perhaps history was not so dull when it was more about uncovering a mystery, and less about learning facts and dates, Runa thought. There was nothing like a present threat to make history seem more relevant.

CHAPTER 7

A knock at the door heralded the server, who led her down through the palace to a room built right into the bedrock of the mountain. The low ceiling pressed upon shelves and shelves of books and scrolls. Runa could not help contrasting it with the library at Orr, so beloved by Eleos, with its high windows and rows of beautifully bound books.

A sneeze came from behind one of the bookshelves, and a thin-faced woman squinted around the end of the shelf at Runa.

"May I help you?" she asked. She held a large book open in front of her, like a shield.

"Yes, at least, I hope so. I was wondering if you have any of the early letters or diaries of King tSardin."

The librarian narrowed her eyes even further and stepped out from behind the shelf. Her hair was tied beneath a green scarf, and she wore a dusty brown robe.

"We don't allow Callenlasians access to private royal documents," she said, snapping shut the book in her hands, turning to leave.

"I'm from Feldemoore," Runa said, with her most disarming smile. "I'm just visiting for a couple of days, and I'm very interested in the history of King tSardin, and my own ancestor, King Felden."

Like a shaft of sunlight falling through a window, Runa had a sudden glimpse of why Elior might have chosen her instead of one of his Callenlasian riders.

The librarian considered with pursed lips, while Runa's heart thudded. What if she was to be refused at the first attempt, after flying all this way?

"Well, I suppose," the librarian demurred, looking at Runa suspiciously. "Usually, a permit is required from one of the Queen's Masters."

"I'm in rather a hurry," Runa tried her most persuasive voice. "Ambassador Rellian assured me that you would be helpful. I only have two days ..."

To Runa's relief, the librarian briskly nodded her head.

"Sit here." She gestured to a row of wooden trestle tables set against the wall. "I'll fetch what we have."

Runa sat on a wooden bench and shivered. Above ground, the Day-Star's heat could be ferocious; here in the depths of the palace the air was as cold as the stone which contained it.

She waited for a long time, listening to distant shuffling and mutterings, wondering how long she could maintain the pretence of being in tSama for personal reasons. With servers and librarians Runa could feign an innocent interest in the history of tSardia. Queen Junal, however, would know what Runa was really looking for. Once she discovered that Runa was digging into the history of the division, her access to the library would certainly be restricted. Junal might even accuse her of treachery and try to arrest her.

Runa drew a calming breath and put on a smile.

At last, the librarian reappeared, bearing a dusty chest. It was a box of polished cedar wood, the kind Runa's father used for his important letters and documents.

"This is the first King's private correspondence from that period," the librarian said.

"Thank you," Runa replied. "Oh – " she added. "I wonder ... can you tell me anything about the Watchers of Callenlas?"

The librarian did not quite roll her eyes, but she certainly walked away with a disgruntled air.

Runa found the catch on the box and lifted the lid. She felt new appreciation for the librarian's scarf as a cloud of dust flew up causing her to splutter and cough. The lid fell against the wall behind the box with a crash. Runa winced at the sound, glancing at the door. She lifted the first few papers out with exaggerated care. At least there were no open windows to blow the fragile documents all over the library.

She sifted through some lists of military equipment and plans for various buildings, before the librarian pushed a small book onto the table at Runa's elbow.

Encyclopaedia of Callenlas, Runa read. The book was old, and quite dusty.

"Thank you!" she called to the bookshelves. There was no reply.

Runa opened the book and searched through the alphabetised list until she found 'Watcher'.

The Watchers of Callenlas were established
some fifty years after the departure of King
Elior, for the purpose of watching for his return.
What began as a small community, living on the
eastern coast, expanded to twelve towers built
from the very north to the south of the island,
each with their own community of Watchers.
The Watchers removed themselves from
ordinary life, and sought to be self-sufficient,
growing or foraging for all their needs, and
spending their free time either watching for
Elior's return, studying the law of the King, or
Sending to him, pleading with him to return.

Runa sat back a little. Lorien must have belonged to one of those communities, and that was where Ilfian had gone also, when he left Orr.

The Watchers were disbanded once King Elior
returned in the five-hundred-and-twenty-
first year of the stars.

So that was why she had not heard of them. They had existed only for the first three-hundred years that Elior had spent in the east.

One mystery solved, Runa drew her attention back to the box of tSardin's letters. It was strange to think he had handled the box, used it daily perhaps, even written some of the pages in her hands, this man who had caused so much trouble to King Elior and his people.

For an hour, Runa turned over letters, papers, documents ... but nothing shed any new light on the division of the kingdom, nor the missing document from King Arten. As the time passed, Runa's anxiety grew. News travelled fast in palaces, especially news about visitors. Runa kept waiting for guards to burst through the doors and haul her away, or at least for the server to announce that she had spent too much time in the library and was required by the Queen.

Runa rubbed the bridge of her nose, frustrated and disappointed. She had thought that if anyone had been working secretly for tSardin at Orr, there might be a letter or a clue to their identity at least, in his private papers.

A final letter lay at the bottom of the box, and Runa unfolded it without thinking, rubbing her neck with her left hand. The handwriting was familiar ... slanting, thick lines ...

Brother,

I write to formally congratulate you on your marriage, though in truth I am astonished. What led you to choose Eleos? I never thought you had any feeling for her, beyond basic kindness. I always thought you and Istria were more of a match.

I care deeply for Eos, and, truth be told, had considered whether she might not be happy with me some day. You must not hurt her. She is beautiful, tSardin, beautiful of soul, I mean – there is a goodness in her that is rarely found. She bears the light of Elior within, I am sure of it. Her goodness is something you and I may only aspire to. Do not ruin her. Do nothing to put out that light, or I will never forgive you, and nor will Elior.

Ilfian

There was a hole in the paper, Runa realised, a thin sliver of a cut, as if tSardin's anger had driven a knife or dagger through it as it lay on a desk.

Ilfian had loved Eleos, then, and tSardin too if he had married her? Though the nasty thought sidled into Runa's mind that tSardin may have married

51

Eleos to spite his brother, knowing Ilfian was favoured over him; or perhaps simply to win the support of the Marsh-Reif in his war for the throne.

Runa looked into the bottom of the box. There were some scraps of paper and dust in the corners, but no clues as to who might have been working for tSardin in Callenlas.

Would it be stealing, Runa wondered, to take the letter to her room? As long as the letter remained in the palace it would only be borrowing, surely.

The librarian was nowhere to be seen. Runa laid the letter carefully between the pages of Eleos's diary and slid it into her bag.

As she did so, her hand brushed the cover of Eleos's diary. Runa froze, not wanting to disturb the idea that sidled into her mind. Eleos had been the first Queen of tSardia, Horgin had said. That meant she would have lived here, in tSama. She must have had rooms somewhere in the palace. Perhaps ... Runa's mouth went dry at the thought ... perhaps some of Eleos's things would still be there, forgotten in a chest or desk.

Heart pounding, Runa gathered her things and hurried out of the library.

Chapter 8

Runa knew better than to ask her server to show her to Eleos's old rooms. He had waited outside the library the entire time, more like a guard than guide. Instead, she asked to see one of the palace gardens. Runa idled between the leafy plants, glancing at the server. Maybe he would become bored or distracted. But he kept her in his sights the entire time.

Frustrated, Runa knew she would have to create her own escape. Her experience as a young Princess, watched closely by anxious tutors and nurses, served her well. Stooping as if to examine a flower near the ground, Runa scooped up a small pebble. With an expert flick, she sent the pebble over the server's head so that it skittered against the wall on the far side of the garden.

Startled, the server looked to see what had made the noise. Runa slipped into the palace through the nearest door, hurrying along the passage as quickly as she could before the server could follow her.

If Junal was keeping such a close eye on her now, Runa could not imagine what would happen to her if the Queen discovered the true purpose of her presence in tSama. Glancing over her shoulder, Runa sought out one of the lowest servers in the palace, knowing that anyone following her would never expect her to speak to such a person. It would buy her time, if it did not completely cover her tracks.

"Will you show me to the old palace?" Runa asked. She knew that part of the palace was very old, built even before tSardin became King. He had lived there as a young man, learning how to rule from the Guardian of the South. He would have brought Eleos there as a young bride, while Arten was still alive.

The floor-sweeper seemed quite startled at being spoken to at all and was reluctant to leave her work. A gold coin, glittering in Runa's palm, quickly changed her mind.

Passing through the back rooms, Runa was shown to a servants' door – of course, a floor-sweeper would only know the servants' access. Even better for covering her tracks.

"The old rooms are only used when there are lots of visitors," the floor-sweeper explained, shyly, before disappearing into the palace.

Having made a hasty search of the tower, Runa stood before a door of inlaid wood showing Lealos and its rivers, remarkably similar to the panel from Orr's library. This must be Eleos's old suite. Drawing a deep breath, Runa opened the door, and stepped inside the rooms of the first Queen of tSardia.

Disappointment was her first emotion. The rooms had clearly stood empty and unused for years, and instead of the traces of the old Queen there was only shuttered light and dust, and a heap of old furniture in one corner.

She did not stay in the reception room, for who would keep anything personal in there? Instead, she travelled through a series of rooms to what would have once been a private sitting room and a grand bedchamber. Here, Runa creaked open the shutters. The bright light slanted in, illuminating a tasteful room with turquoise and gilt walls and a pale marble floor. Runa opened the cupboards in a small dressing room, but there was only dust in the corners, and a discarded feather.

Runa looked through the window and found a view over the sea to the south. Two ships were bobbing on the tide, their sails lowered as they drew near the harbour. She felt again the loneliness of the Marsh-Reif's daughter. How had she found life as tSardin's wife, living in the barren heat of the south, when she had come from the Marshes? Runa sank onto a seat built into the large windowsill, and it shifted beneath her weight. It was very old, she realised; and with that her cheeks grew hot. She had been foolish to think she might find anything here after more than two-hundred years. The room had been stripped of Eleos's things long ago, and countless guests had probably stayed there since.

Despite her disappointment and the emptiness of the room, Runa felt a sense of kinship with the long-dead Queen. Perhaps Eleos had sat in this very window, hoping to catch a breeze in the sultry heat of high summer. Runa drew out the slim diary and opened it to read.

Ilfian showed me a book today, poems by someone called Aleifir the Bard. The book is very old, but the poems are beautiful. Ilfian said Watcher Lorien told him about them, and he knew straight away that I would love them too.

My favourite is a poem called "Homesick" and the line "Oh, take me back, before I die, to the land where soft hills lie". It reminded me of Lealos, of home, and it made me cry. Ilfian was so kind. He's not as handsome as tSardin, but he has been kind to me when everyone else ... there, I'm crying again. Perhaps Papa will allow me to return to Lealos for a time in the summer, just to visit.

Runa lowered the book, puzzled. Eleos's feelings for tSardin had made sense; she had married him, after all. But it seemed that Eleos and Ilfian had also formed a connection. She itched to read more, but now was not the time. No doubt she had already raised suspicions by evading her server-guard.

Stepping out of the old suite of royal rooms, Runa found herself face to face with one of the Queen's attendants. Dressed in royal blue satin, with elaborate jewels in her auburn hair, the attendant curtseyed, her eyes fixed upon Runa's.

Runa closed the door behind her and smiled in what she hoped was a disarming way.

"Queen Junal thanks you for your interest in the history of our royal family," the attendant said. "She wishes to remind you that, although you are from Feldemoore, we know where your loyalties lie."

Runa blinked and licked her lips.

"If you have a wish to see the palace, a tour can be arranged by one of the Queen's attendants."

Runa mustered her best princessly tone.

"Please thank your Queen for me," she replied, still smiling stiffly. "And do remind her that King tSardin was also an ancestor of mine."

Runa made to step past the attendant, but the blue robe moved to block her way. Runa's heart sped up.

"The Queen does not want to create enemies, but nor is she afraid of offending those who oppose her, wherever they are from."

Runa stood a little straighter and managed to resist placing her hand on her knife.

"The Queen only wishes to protect the friendship between our people." The attendant's voice was as silken as her robe.

Runa's fingers twitched near her hip.

"Friends don't grasp, or threaten war, however nicely," she wanted to say. "And I don't play games." But instead, thinking of everyone back in Callenlas, she tilted her head in polite acquiescence.

"Of course," she agreed, sweetening the tone of her voice.

Heart pounding, Runa took a large stride, bypassing the attendant. Had she said too much? She resisted looking back; keeping her head tall as she strode towards her room.

CHAPTER 9

Once inside her room, Runa, fighting for calm, leaned against the closed door, and exhaled, shaken by the attendant's threat. The Queen must have been told that Runa had requested tSardin's documents; she must know what Runa was looking for.

Runa glanced at the Day-Star outside her window. It was already past noon, and almost time for her to meet the Queen Junal.

But for now ... Runa shifted over to the bed. Climbing on, she sat upright with her legs crossed and eyes closed. It would take a lot of effort, but she wanted to try to reach Zaphreth.

Sending her mind out, Runa reached across the eastern sea and the lands beyond. Her strength quickly grew thin and faint, despite all her training.

Dizziness threatened to overcome her, and she was about to give up, when she caught that vivid, blue glimmer that she knew was Zaphreth. She called out to him, trying to reach him before her strength gave out.

He did not respond, and she was forced to withdraw, pulling her soul back, back, back until she collapsed onto the bed with a gasp. She thrust her fist into the mattress, frustrated by her weakness in mind arts.

Forcing herself to concentrate on her service to King Elior, Runa tidied up her hair and brushed dust off her tunic and trousers. Too late, she realised that she should have brought another change of clothes. She had grabbed the dress after Master Horgin told her she might be expected to attend a dinner with the Ambassador, but it was not suitable for an informal meeting, even with a Queen. Neither was her tunic.

Before she could decide which outfit would be worse, Ambassador Rellian arrived at the door and took her through the palace to the Queen's chambers. Queen Junal's private receiving room had black marble floors and leafy plants in large, decorated pots standing against the engraved stone walls. Colourful silk curtains drifted in the breeze from the terrace, which looked out over the glittering southern sea. Runa opened her mouth to ask Rellian a question, but the Ambassador shook his head.

"The room is monitored at all times," he muttered in her ear, pretending to show her to a seat.

Runa had only just lowered herself to the padded sofa when a door opened and a stream of attendants, officials and servers entered, followed by a woman who could only be the Queen of tSardia. She was surprisingly short, barely the same height as Runa, with dark hair neatly arranged, and a haughty expression on her youthful face. She was not especially beautiful, but her features were even, and her appearance was made striking by her clothes. Her robe of viridian satin flowed to her feet, and her bare arms were decorated with bracelets and jewelled cuffs.

Runa curtseyed, which always proved an interesting experience in her tunic and trousers. The Queen's dark eyes flicked up and down, and her lip curled slightly in disdain.

Straightening her shoulders, Runa reminded herself of her status. She was a servant of King Elior, and a Princess of Feldemoore, and that was that. Still, she had to fight the urge to raise her hand to run through her copper hair to tweak out a few tangles.

"I must give my condolences and congratulations to you, Queen Junal," Runa said, sweeping a second bow, referring to the loss of her father, the King.

"Thank you."

Junal sat on one of the padded couches and gestured for Runa to sit also. Attendants stepped forward, bowing, and laid silver trays of food and drink on the ornate table between them.

"I understand that you are a good friend of King Elior?" Queen Junal's voice was calm and soothing; however inexperienced she was in ruling, she had been taught impeccable manners. Yet Runa knew she was stepping on quicksand as she answered.

"Yes, your majesty."

"I trust you found what you were looking for, in my archives?"

The Queen's dark eyes met Runa's directly, and Runa's insides squirmed.

"Your librarian was very helpful, your majesty," Runa answered. "I learned a lot about the Watchers of Callenlas."

The Queen's eyebrow lifted. Runa shifted on her seat and reached for a silver cup of wine. Why had the King chosen her for this mission? She lacked all the elegance and grace of the Queen and had never been a diplomat; it was like sending a horse into an apothecary.

"I do not want a war," the Queen said, in her clear, soft voice. "I simply want a recognition of the mistake made by the council of Callenlas when my ancestor tSardin, was forced from his rightful throne."

Runa glanced at the Ambassador who appeared to be Sending, his eyes closed, his fingers steepled against his chest. Perhaps he was imploring King Elior to send a more experienced diplomat.

"I believe King Elior would say that no mistake was made," Runa ventured. She felt as though she was standing on the edge of a cliff, and the Queen was levelling a sword at her throat. One false word and she would be tipped over the edge, taking all of Callenlas with her.

"I have heard it all before." Queen Junal swept aside the arguments of the centuries with one delicate flick of her wrist. "'The laws of Callenlas state that King Elior may appoint whomever he wishes to be King.'"

"Prince," Runa corrected instinctively.

"Excuse me?"

"The rulers of Callenlas are Princes," Runa repeated. "They rule as representatives of the only King, Elior, your majesty," she added.

The Queen's lips compressed, and Runa wished she had held her tongue. Perhaps the King had sent her because she was a woman, hoping she could get on the side of the young Queen and befriend her. If that was the case, he had chosen poorly again. Runa could never help speaking her mind.

"Nevertheless," Junal said, her tone sweeter than ever, "the fact remains that no will exists signed by King Arten, or Elior, leaving the throne to Ilfian, and therefore, by default, the throne should have gone to tSardin, or now, to his current living heir."

The Queen selected a stuffed date from one of the trays and planted it in her mouth.

Runa glanced again at the Ambassador, who shrugged. It was over. Runa would have no more access to the library of tSama.

Well, Runa thought, it was all or nothing now.

"My Queen," Runa said. "Your people have suffered greatly from repeated wars over many centuries. King Elior is eager to extend friendship towards you. My own land, Feldemoore, has benefitted greatly from his wisdom, help and protection."

A disdainful smile crept onto the Queen's lips. Runa ploughed on.

"Meretheos also, has been involved in various councils and efforts to bring peace and unity to our island."

"King Elior," Junal said in a louder voice, preventing Runa from continuing, "claims to care very much about doing what is right. Well, I also care about what is right." She leaned forwards, her dark eyes fixed earnestly on Runa's. "I care deeply about my people. I care about what is right and good for them. I do not want a war, only justice."

"Have you ever seen war?" Runa asked, softly. "I have. I do not think it is ever worth the cost."

The Queen's face closed, and she stood.

"It is such a shame that you will have to return to Feldemoore tomorrow," she said. "Our banquets are famous."

Runa swallowed hard as the Queen swept out. She had failed.

CHAPTER 10

Runa stepped out of the Queen's private chambers and blew out a lungful of air.

"Care deeply," she muttered to herself bitterly, remembering the field of bodies she had walked through the last time tSardia had asserted its claim to Callenlas. Whatever Junal said, war was where this would end, if she persisted.

Runa stepped to a window and looked out over the roofs of tSama. The southern heat of the Day-Star beat upon white walls and flat roofs, narrow streets and crowded market squares. Beyond the walls, the rugged slopes of the southern mountains stood like the grey edge of a knife against a vivid blue sky. The sheer mountainsides held jagged caves where wild dragons still lurked, though they were becoming rarer now.

Why did you send me? she Sent desperately, across the miles of land and ocean between herself and Elior. She knew she could not cover the distance herself; when Sending with the King he reached over the miles and found her. But she believed he would hear; somehow, he always did.

"Let me show you back to your room, my Princess," Ambassador Rellian said, coming up behind her. He was trying to hide his disappointment. Perhaps he was as bewildered as Runa as to why King Elior had sent an inelegant Feldemoorian Princess to navigate such a difficult situation.

Runa followed him back to her room in silence. She would have no more access to the library, or any other documents that might have been helpful. In the morning, she would be escorted to the dragon caves and sent on her way, her mission to prevent the war aborted.

Back in her room, Runa shuffled through the papers Master Horgin had given her. Shaking herself free of the Queen's threat, made all the more sinister by its saccharine delivery, Runa turned her attention back to Eleos. The old Queen had begun to feel like a friend, especially now that she had seen her rooms. Though her mission was over, Runa still felt drawn to the story of the unlikely first Queen of tSardia. She opened the diary once again, turning to one of the later pages.

Ilfian has gone.

I don't think I really believed he would actually go … I thought he was just talking about becoming a Watcher. But Master Lorien was released from his duties to return to Navador, and Ilfian went with him.

He did not even come to see me. He Sent to me, from the road, to tell me what he was doing, and begged me to say nothing until his father had read his letter. It took everything in me to hide what I was feeling from him. But my heart is breaking.

It's not so much him leaving – I think I could bear that, though I do not know what I will do without him to talk to, and Lorien gone as well. It is that he left without thinking of me. I was an afterthought.

And so, I see that I was a fool, and deceived myself. He does not love me as I'd hoped, or at least, the love he once had for me has faded.

He did not mean to deceive me, nor to forget me. I hope he is happy with the Watchers in Navador. I hope he finds what he has been looking for; peace, perhaps, and a purpose beyond politics, which I know he hates.

But I wish he loved me.

Eleos's pain seemed pressed into the ink that curled across the page. Runa fished out the poem written for Eleos and frowned. The handwriting was the same as the letter in tSardin's box. She was sure of it. She searched for the letter and set it side by side with the poem. It was certainly the same handwriting. Ilfian had clearly loved Eos ... but why then, had he left her?

Runa pushed the poem and letter into the diary and closed it firmly. Peoples' feelings changed, that was all.

Runa. Zaphreth's Sending almost made Runa fall off the bed. She startled, as if he had caught her with her own diary laid bare.

Zaphreth, she replied. She felt heat flood her face and was glad he could not see her.

Did you Send to me earlier? His presence was a thin, azure cloud on the fringe of her consciousness.

I tried, she said. *You're still much better at it than me.*

His laugh flickered in her mind like a flame.

What are you doing in tSama? It took me ages to find you.

I'm on a mission for King Elior. How are you?

She felt strangely anxious, and a small part of her mind hoped there wasn't still dust in her hair from the library. Then she shook her head at herself; Zaphreth could not know that through Sending.

Busy, came the wry reply. *Did you need something?*

Yes, you, thought Runa, crossly, but she managed to keep the thought in check, and did not Send it.

The new Queen is resurrecting the tSardian claim to the throne of Callenlas, Runa explained. *I'm here to research the division of the kingdom, though I don't think Elior has chosen well.*

He always chooses well, Zaphreth interjected.

Anyway, I wondered if you knew anything about that time, anything that might help prove that the throne was left to Ilfian, not tSardin? Runa rushed her words, realising as she Sent that Zaphreth was not likely to know any more than she did; she had simply wanted an excuse to reach out to him. He would see it, surely he would. He had always been good at reading her.

There was a long pause, so long that Runa began to think Zaphreth had become too tired to reach her and had abandoned the conversation.

I don't know anything about that, really.

Oh. Runa knew she should let Zaphreth go, but it had been so long since they had spoken. *The King thought there might have been someone on tSardin's side, working against Ilfian from within Orr, someone who destroyed the King's will leaving the throne to Ilfian. I thought you might know who that could be? Was there anyone who served King tSardin in the early days?*

Not that I can remember. I didn't really study that period much in our training, and what I was told when I was in tSardia is probably unreliable.

Runa felt embarrassed by her own desperation in trying to reach Zaphreth.

I have to go, Zaphreth said. *Mielle is waiting.*

Mielle?

The daughter of the Governor here. Well, they don't really have Governors; they call them Olats. Mielle was going to show me the fountain gardens.

Lovely. You're clearly very busy so ...

She felt the knife of regret in the tone of her Sending.

If someone did destroy any documents, it would have to be someone very close to Prince Ilfian, someone with access to his private papers, who could enter his room unquestioned. Take care, Runa.

Take care yourself, she returned, but he had gone.

Runa groaned and fell back, careless of the fragile, historical documents that littered her bed. Who was this *Mielle* person, and why was she showing Zaphreth around a fountain garden of all places? Since when were fountains so interesting to Zaphreth?

Runa pressed her hands over her face. Zaphreth had been gone for four years and was not likely to be returning soon. The tiny hope she had allowed herself once had been brutally crushed, and it was time she let it go.

Chapter 11

Runa had never been able to tolerate boredom. With her hopes of searching for King Arten's will in ruins, she still had an entire evening to fill before she could fly back to Callenlas. She was surprised to feel disappointment as she opened Eleos's diary and found she had only a few pages left.

My wedding is tomorrow. King Arten and my father have made it very clear how delighted they are. I am glad to have brought some good to them, but I am sad to be moving further away from my beloved Lealos. I begged Papa to allow me to return for this final summer, for once I am in the south with tSardin it will be harder than ever for me to go home. But he said I must stay, and perhaps he was right, for the summer has been busy with dress fittings and lessons in how to be a good wife to the crown Prince.

I will close this diary tonight, and that will be the end of my childhood. I am eighteen; it is time I became a woman. I will write my heart here, and then close the book, and I will not think of it again. The next diary I write will be as a wife. Oh, I am afraid. How can I, little Eos, be the wife of the future King of Callenlas? I am so afraid that tSardin is only marrying me because his father is pressing for it. He was made Governor of the south two years ago, and I have not seen him since, until he arrived at Orr last week; and we have both been so busy since that we have hardly spoken. He is not the boy I knew; his time in the south has changed him. He is broader, quite formidable in fact, and his face is that of a man. He acknowledged me formally, but the twinkle that used to be in his eye has gone.

I used to like him once, as a girl likes a boy. Will I love him as a woman to a man? Will he love me? Does love matter at all when we are all just pieces in a game of Cities? The King and Queen are pleased, and so we must be also.

I will love tSardin. I will love him back to himself. He always had a soft spot for me. He will listen, in time, I am sure.

Istria is furious. She is meant to help bear my train in the wedding tomorrow and I am quite sure she means to drop it at some point. She cannot say that she is furious, especially in front of the King and Queen, but I know she had hoped to marry tSardin herself, not for love, but because she wants to be Queen someday. I cannot help feeling a little triumph that tSardin chose me, and not her. I am not foolish enough to think he finds me more beautiful or clever; I know it is simply that my father is offering military support to King Arten. But still, I am tSardin's bride, not Istria.

Istria is to come to tSama with me, as one of my attendants. I don't think either of us are especially pleased by the arrangement. I had asked for Morival, but Istria's father wishes her to be near him again, and I suppose it makes more sense this way.

Morival sides with Istria, as she always has. She seems to think King Arten and her father are negotiating for her to marry Felden. I do not think either of them are especially thrilled about it.

I find it so strange to think of us all, playing together, learning in the library, playing tricks on our tutors ... we always knew that we were here for bigger purposes, part of our parents' plans. But now I am to be married, and I feel as though we have all turned on each other, and I don't even know why.

And Ilfian ... I cannot even write his name. I should not, really, but I must, and then I will close this book and it will all be forgotten. I read his poem again just now, the one he wrote for me in the summer when he was seventeen. The only person who really saw me, and, I believe, once loved me. Even now he has not returned from Navador, and so I must conclude that his love has truly died. I think, if he still loved me, he would have come back and asked me not to marry tSardin.

So, I put his poem away, and I will leave it in Orr, with my diary, hidden in my windowsill

in the library. Perhaps, when I am Queen,
I will find it again and laugh at myself for my
childish romance.

Oh tSardin, I hope we will be happy together.
May Elior and the stars bless our marriage.

Threads of thought tangled in Runa's head. Why had Ilfian remained in Navador if he loved Eleos so much? Had tSardin really loved Eleos, or just married her to please their parents? Had Morival married Felden? She did not think so.

Runa scoured her memory for history lessons from years ago, in the library at Lorandia. Felden had been the founder of her land, the first King of Feldemoore ... One dreadful winter Runa had been forced to learn her entire genealogy, from Felden all the way to King Mabrigas and Queen Elliel. Felden had been the first name ... but she was sure his wife had been Adriel of Globe.

What had happened to Morival, then?

Runa shuffled through the papers and found a slim volume tucked among them.

A *History of the Division of the Kingdom* by Felligin of Bray.

Perhaps I should have started with this, Runa thought wryly. She flicked open the pages and found a rather dreary account, the kind of book she had been forced to study as a child. Wrinkling her nose, Runa turned towards the end, finding a section with the title, "The Marriage of Prince Ilfian and Lady Morival". Ilfian! Morival had married Ilfian?

Runa scanned the paragraph.

The Prince and Lady Morival were married three months after the end of the war, after the burial of Queen Eleos ...

"What?" Runa exclaimed, aloud. She turned back a few pages.

In an added tragedy, only six weeks after the declared truce, news reached tSardin that his wife, Lady Eleos of the Marshes, the first Queen of tSardia, had died. Though she had been ill for some time, her death came as a shock to the Prince, for the Lady was only twenty-one.

At the time, rumours abounded that the Lady had been poisoned, but it ill behooves us to listen to idle tales, and we only

*concern ourselves with substantiated fact
in this volume.*

"What?" Runa repeated. She stared at the scattered papers, wondering where to begin. Eleos had died? Morival had married Ilfian ...

Slowly, an idea came turning into her mind, like the creaking of a large mill wheel. *The next diary I write will be as a wife,* Runa recalled Eleos's final diary entry. Eleos had begun another diary once she lived in tSama as tSardin's wife. And since Istria was with her, Eleos must have once again felt compelled to hide it ...

Runa glanced outside. The Day-Star was already well on its way towards the horizon, its colour deepening as evening approached. She did not have long, but if there was something of Eleos's left in her old rooms, she had to find it. It might mention who was working for tSardin, or even hold some proof that Arten had left the throne to Ilfian, not tSardin. It was her last chance.

Stuffing papers, diary, books and all into her bag, Runa slipped out of her room. The old royal suite was in another part of the palace altogether, and she had to concentrate hard to remember the way. After turning into several unfamiliar rooms and backtracking, Runa became aware of soft footsteps on the tiles behind her and the swish of silk against the floor. As delicate as the Queen's attendant was, she was no good at tracking.

Runa deliberately stepped into a wrong room and ducked into a deep window recess. Peering around the curtains, she grimaced to herself as that royal blue robe rustled in through the door after her. Runa pressed her face to the window. Tantalisingly, she could see the tower where the old royal rooms lay, just on the other side of a square garden terrace below.

The attendant had stopped, hands on hips, looking this way and that inside the room for any trace of Runa. With the utmost care, Runa lifted the latch on the tall, glass window and eased it open. Hardly daring to breathe, she slipped through the gap and out onto the narrow roof that sloped down towards the leaves of a tree. Runa crept along the roof. Pausing at the end of the wall, she risked a glance inside and smothered a snigger as the attendant lifted the lid on a large chest, and peered inside a massive vase.

There was no time to enjoy her triumph further. With a grunt of effort, Runa scrambled up onto a wall that ran between two gardens to join the old royal tower. She was perilously high, looking down over the roofs and gardens of the palace. She could even see the dragon caves, just on the outskirts of the palace, a series of cuts made into the rock where the Queen's fleet, and Shari of course, were stabled.

Catlike, Runa ran along the wall, making for a window in the tower. She found it locked. The second window along was open a crack, but it was a long way from the wall.

Runa could hear movement in one of the rooms letting onto the garden. How would she explain herself if anyone found her climbing the walls of tSama? Being from Feldemoore could only carry her so far.

She would have to risk the jump over the courtyard, two dizzying floors below, to the further window.

Voices were coming now, servants chattering on their way into the garden behind Runa.

With a gulp, Runa leapt.

CHAPTER 12

Picking herself up, Runa held still, listening for anyone who had heard her fall. Teetering on the window ledge, she had strained to open the window, stiff with years of disuse. When it gave, she rolled into the room, thudding against bare, dusty floorboards.

Hurrying through the tower to Eleos's bedroom, Runa dropped her bag on the floor and began searching. She pushed each tile, pressed all the panels on the walls, and even stuck her head up the chimney, bringing down a rain of soot. Sneezing, Runa shook her head free of dust, and stared around the room. How long did she have before the attendant found her? What would the Queen do to her, then?

Runa searched the dressing room but found nothing there either. Anxiety pounded in her head. Either Eleos's diary must have been destroyed or it had never existed at all. Perhaps Eleos felt it was too risky to write her private thoughts down, especially with Istria nosing through her possessions.

Hands on her head in desperation, Runa sank down onto the ancient seat below the window and felt it shift again, almost imperceptibly, as it had before. Such an old room, she thought. Then she turned, pushing again on the threadbare cushion and felt that tiny shift of the seat beneath.

Runa pulled the cushion aside, her heart hammering in her throat. A wooden ledge lay beneath, set flush to the stone wall. Runa pressed it, and it tilted. Runa pried her fingers under the rim of the seat and tugged. The wooden seat creaked forward. Grimacing, Runa gripped it and pulled hard. Suddenly it gave way, and she stumbled backwards, the entire ledge in her hands.

In the stone of the windowsill lay a very thin cavity, only the depth of her thumb or even less. But it was enough room for a small book, and a sheaf of papers.

Runa punched the air and set the seat aside. The book was like the other journal; a little larger and thinner, but plain calfskin dyed a pale blue, faded and stained with age. Runa picked it up and turned it over. The brittle pages turned with a rustle, revealing Eleos's neat, unmistakable handwriting.

The creak of a door lower in the tower made Runa jump. She glanced into the seat and snatched up the papers that had lain beneath the diary, stuffing all into her bag. As she replaced the seat and cushion and closed the shutters, she tried not to imagine Master Horgin's horror at her careless treatment of historic documents.

Holding her breath, Runa crept towards the Lealos door, straining to hear the attendant. The cawing of gulls came softly from beyond the windows, and the soft shushing of the sea, but Runa could also hear the sinister sweep of satin robes on dusty floors.

The door opened abruptly, and Runa only just managed to slide behind it as the attendant swept in. She moved rapidly into the next room, allowing Runa to slip out of the door and hurry through the tower to the servants' exit.

Too anxious to feel triumphant, Runa began to find her way through the palace to her rooms. She wanted to return as quickly as she could, but the palace was a maze. At last, she found the familiar door and unlocked it. Shoving the bag under her bed, Runa shook the dust from her hair and drew several breaths, forcing herself to be calm.

Only moments afterwards, a soft knock came at her door. Runa opened it with a bright smile.

The attendant's face registered surprise and confusion; clearly, she had expected to find Runa's room empty.

"Does the Queen command my presence?" Runa asked, suppressing her heaving chest.

"No," the attendant replied. "She told me to offer you that tour of the palace."

Runa nodded with a regretful smile.

"As much as I'd enjoy that," she replied, "I really had hoped to have an early night, ready for my long journey home tomorrow. I'm sure the Queen understands the importance of beauty sleep."

Despite the seriousness of the situation, Runa almost laughed – 'the importance of beauty sleep' was not a phrase she ever thought she'd say.

But the attendant simply nodded and hesitated on the threshold.

"Good evening," Runa said, and shut the door.

She let out the air burning in her lungs and moved to the bed, making it creak as if she was lying down on it. It was some time before the attendant's footsteps moved away from the door, but at last Runa felt able to fish her bag out and look at the things she had found.

She opened the diary first, for Eleos might have known who was helping tSardin. She wanted to read from the beginning, and understand Eleos's story better, but she had only a short time before her departure.

Runa turned towards the end of the book.

I have pleaded with tSardin, begged on my knees for him to abandon his terrible ambition. But pride and anger rule him now; he will not listen. He pushed me against the wall, slapped my face, and told me to cease whinging and help him.

I passed Istria in the hall on my way back to my room. She smiled at me, so triumphant, so scathing. I know what she thinks of me, whatever she pretends to my face. I know she has tSardin wrapped around her little finger. I know she was on her way to see him.

I am so afraid, but who can I turn to? I am all alone here in the stone walls of tSama. I cannot write, for my letters will be intercepted. I have tried to Send to Guardian Rhemos, but my mind is weak. I have spent hours Sending to King Elior, and I do not understand why he does not come to help.

I think Istria is making me ill. I have been weak and in pain for so long, and I grow more and more ill. I have headaches every day, and all I can do is lie on my bed and wait for the pain to pass.

I fear Istria. I have asked for her to be removed, but tSardin says it would be an insult to her father. He laughed when I said I thought she was poisoning me. I am not sure it is poison; I fear it is magic of some kind, but I am certain she means me harm.

Runa frowned. Would Istria really do something as awful as murder Eleos? Turning the page, she found Eleos echoing her thoughts.

*tSardin has ridden north with his army.
I think my heart will break. How have we
all descended to this? Ilfian, tSardin, Felden
and Erchen – we used to play together. Even
Istria, who never liked me … I never imagined
she would be capable of such hardness and
ambition, nor such unkindness to me.*

The final entry was unusually untidy, as though
Eleos struggled to hold the pen.

*A messenger has just come to me, from
Guardian Rhemos personally. Istria tried
to keep him from me, saying I was too ill to
receive him, but I heard the dispute from my
bed and insisted the man be brought in. I had
to dismiss my attendants quite forcefully.*

*Rhemos wants me to speak to tSardin, but
my husband is already on his way north. Could
I follow him? I am so ill, but perhaps I can try.*

*Istria will try to stop me, but she does
not know how strong I am. I can be stubborn
when it matters. And what matters more than
Elior's kingdom?*

I will go. It may be what kills me, but I will plead with tSardin to end this war.

The diary ended. Runa turned the remaining pages, but all were blank.

She set the book down in her lap. The Day-Star was sinking in a pool of blood-red light, and her chamber was bathed in crimson.

Runa glanced at the papers she had retrieved with the diary, perhaps letters from Eleos's mother. One was a sketch, a drawing of Lealos, the town surrounded by water, a fleet of boats waiting at the quay. Runa was quite sure that Eleos had drawn it, perhaps one idle evening, longing for home.

The second paper was stiff and weighty, like the paper her father used for official documents. It was heavy to lift, and when Runa unfolded it, she was puzzled to find four wax seals at the bottom of the paper.

Then she gasped. The paper was signed by Guardian Rhemos, two other councillors of Callenlas, and lastly, in a wavering hand, by King Arten.

Runa scanned the page, her heart thudding loudly. It was clearly written in haste, without the usual care given to official documents, the pen marks brisk, and several words misspelled and then crossed out and rewritten.

> I, Arten, Prince of Callenlas and all her islands, do hereby declare that my son, Ilfian, is to be crowned Prince upon my death, by the will of King Elior, and by the agreement of the Guardians of Callenlas, and according to the will of the council of the King.

Folded in with the document was a letter, also hurriedly written.

> My dear Eleos,
>
> I write to you with great urgency. It is imperative that this message and the document with it be kept absolutely secret. You must trust no one, not even those you consider close friends. There are even some among Prince Ilfian's council who are acting against him and King Elior.
>
> My dear, I am sure tSardin has explained to you that Prince Arten has long intended to leave the throne to Ilfian. We discussed it with them several years ago when they were boys.

Prince Arten cherished a hope that tSardin would mature, and let go of his ambition and pride, but sadly we have seen no evidence of it.

The sudden accident which befell Prince Arten forced him to commit his intention to writing. I sat with him and wrote the words contained in the will, and we had a copy made. The Prince signed them both, as did I, and his councillors. I have one among the official papers in the Prince's private room; and this one I send to you, my dear, in the hope that you will be able to dissuade your husband from his intended war.

If he sees that the decision is confirmed and officially supported, I hope it will bring an end to his ambitions, and peace to our land.

I know you are dear to him; you endeared yourself to each of the Princes. I hope with all my heart that he will listen to you.

Rhemos

The paper trembled in Runa's hands. Frustration seethed inside her – the diary held no more information about Eleos's last days, and clearly the Guardian's hope that tSardin would be dissuaded from war had failed. The terrible battle had been fought where the desert now lay. Ilfian had won, and drove his brother back into the south, but the cost in lives had been terrible, and the kingdom had been torn apart, undoing Elior's hard-won peace.

Knowing the years of pain that one man's ambition and hunger for power had brought to so many, it was with sadness as well as relief that Runa closed her eyes and Sent to the King.

I found it.

CHAPTER 13

Riding north, with Shari's wings catching a warm updraught from the tSardian coast, Runa found she could breathe again. She had forgotten how miserable it was to be tangled in politics. She was looking forward to going back to her work as a skyrider in Callenlas and Feldemoore.

The Queen had viewed the document in stony silence when the Ambassador laid it upon her table.

"It is a fake," she pronounced coolly, after a pause.

"It cannot be, my Queen," the Ambassador said. "The Princess Runa discovered it in Queen Eleos's apartments."

"She is lying!" the Queen exclaimed, her dark eyes flashing at Runa.

Runa simply lifted her eyebrow. To accuse a Princess of lying was the height of indecency, and the Queen knew it. Her rosy lips pressed together until they were white, and she stormed from the room.

The document was locked in a chest, strapped firmly to Shari's back behind Runa. It would be stored in Orr, under the highest security, for it silenced any claims tSardia might ever make to the throne of Callenlas.

Banking slightly to correct their course towards Orr, Runa mused on the history she had rediscovered. As relieved as she was to have averted a war, she was still puzzling over some questions: who had destroyed the official copy of King Arten's decree? And why had the two northern kingdoms been created?

Arriving in Orr, as twilight descended over the capital, Runa left Shari with a trusted fellow skyrider, and took the box straight to the library and Master Horgin. He took the box with reverence and locked it in a secret cupboard, which he would not even show to Runa. She had to wait, looking around at the carvings so beloved of Eleos, until the Master of Histories returned.

"The other papers?" he asked anxiously. Runa grinned. She took her bag off her shoulder and unpacked the papers and letters Horgin had lent her.

"They got a bit mixed up," she explained apologetically, seeing the Master's face fall.

"Ah, no matter," he said sadly, pressing out the creases in one of the letters.

"I was wondering," Runa said, "how the two northern kingdoms came to be? I know Felden became King of Feldemoore, of course, and Erchen King of Meretheos, but ... I never read about any wars."

"That's because there were none," Master Horgin said. He was already looking through the letters, laying them out on the table, trying to put them back into chronological order. "The two younger brothers came to Ilfian after the war with tSardin was settled and asked for lands of their own. Ilfian could not bear another war, so he reluctantly agreed to peacefully divide the kingdom with his brothers. Here," he added, selecting a letter from one of the piles on the table, and offered it to Runa.

She took it and read, in the soft lamplight:

Erchen, brother,

Enclosed you will find my decree that the lands from the northern coast to the Amaris River, and from the Drogor Isles to the Pass of Uri, will belong to you and your posterity, and that Callenlas relinquishes all claim upon them. If this satisfies you, bring it to Orr and we will sign it together, with the council bearing witness.

I make one request of you, however. Eleos came from the Marshes, which will now pass into your hands. Will you name your land for her, in the stars' tongue: Meretheos (Eos's Land)? I know she was dear to you, as she was to us all. I cannot think of a better way for her name to be commemorated. I am quite sure tSardin will now marry Istria, and Eos's name will otherwise be forgotten.

Your brother, Ilfian

"He loved her," Runa whispered softly. "Why didn't he come back from Navador and stop her from marrying tSardin?"

"He did not hear of the marriage until it was too late," Horgin muttered, peering at one letter. "The

Watchers sometimes took vows of seclusion, hoping to better hear King Elior's voice without distraction. Ilfian took such a vow, and a series of letters and messages piled up while he was in the tower. It was only after he finished the time of his vow that he learned of Eleos's marriage to tSardin. He married the Lady Morival, you know, partly to ensure the help of the tree-dwellers in his war against tSardin."

"It's tragic," Runa said.

Master Horgin fished out another letter.

"You might want to read this."

"It's from Elior," Runa exclaimed, recognising the writing instantly.

"Indeed."

Runa took the letter aside and sat on a dusty bench under a towering bookcase to read it. She squinted in the dim orange light.

Dearest Ilfian,

Please accept my apologies for writing, rather than Sending. I know this will have taken several weeks to reach you, and perhaps during that delay your feelings of despair will have grown. But I wanted you to be able to read my words again and again, through the years, if necessary, and have them sink deeply into your heart. If I had Sent you may have only half-remembered them or remembered them differently.

I know your despair, Ilfian. I know you feel you have failed. I grieve with you for tSardin's fall into darkness, and for your other brothers' greed. I grieve for the war, and how human beings fall into violence and division so easily.

I also know how faithfully you have served me during these troubled times. You have not sought violence but peace. Yet when all other remedies had been exhausted, you took up your blade and showed immense courage in riding out against your brother. You did the best you could in a terrible situation, against people who had long closed their ears to the wisdom of the stars.

You are weary now, Ilfian, and discouraged. Things have not ended as you had hoped or imagined. But that is not a mark of failure. A man who has loved and lived by my light, has not failed.

You will be remembered as Ilfian the Peacemaker, and I can think of no better title for a Prince of Callenlas.

I also know how much you loved Eleos, and how you grieve for her. She was badly treated by tSardin and Istria, and it will not be forgotten by the Council of the Stars. But you must not grieve for her too deeply. No one who bears the light of the stars can truly die. Her soul will be welcomed into the Fields of Light, and she will never again know pain or suffering. You will see her again, when your own journey under the Day-Star is done.

Rule by my light, Ilfian, and keep it always with you. Listen to Guardian Rhemos; he is my faithful servant.

Elior

Runa closed the letter. She could not shake a sense of tragedy, despite King Elior's words. No one's story seemed to have ended well; Eleos died, possibly murdered by Istria; tSardin succumbed to darkness; even her own ancestor, Felden, with his brother Erchen, had descended to greed and ambition by asking for their own lands; and Ilfian, in spite of all his efforts, had ended up with a divided kingdom and a political marriage.

"What happened to Istria?" Runa asked, handing the letter back to the Master of Histories.

"After Queen Eleos died, everyone expected tSardin to marry her," he explained, easing the letter into one of his stacks. "But ... he seemed to turn against her. There were many rumours that the Queen died at her hand, though there is no evidence to support the accusations. King tSardin ended up marrying the Lady Leno, daughter of the Guardian of the South. It is their descendants who now rule tSardia."

Runa left the library and returned to the room she always used when she stayed at Orr. She was weary, suddenly, to her bones, from travelling, and politics, and the power games played by people, and, ultimately, the darkness that seemed to thrive in every human soul. When tSardia attacked Callenlas ten years before, it had been the dark star Lur driving the aggression, but the division of the kingdom showed that human beings were capable of a darkness all their own.

It was the middle of the night when Runa sat up abruptly. It took her a moment to find her bearings ... was she at home in Lorandia? Back at Orr? Or still within the oppressive walls of tSama? The moonlight filtering through the window landed on her rumpled tunic thrown over a chair, and the walls of a small guest room in Orr. Runa relaxed.

Despite her weariness, sleep had not come easily. She had spent hours turning everything over in her mind; questions left unresolved by the books and papers Master Horgin had provided.

"Morival," she thought, her mind racing. "I bet it was Morival who destroyed Ilfian's copy of King Arten's will!"

Zaphreth had said it had to be someone close to Ilfian, someone who could access his private room unquestioned. It had to be Morival, who had always been so desperate for Istria's friendship.

A bitter taste rose in Runa's mouth. Poor Ilfian, betrayed by his own brother and wife. But foolish man, he could have had Eleos's love, had he just ...

Runa drew a deep breath and pressed her hands to her eyes.

My King, she Sent softly, into the night, trusting he would hear her frail Sending across the miles. He always did. *My King ... please, could I be given leave? I would like to visit Zaphreth.*

His answer came at dawn, while she was still half-asleep.

I have an important mission for you, his voice nudged her awake. *I need you to fly to Embassa for me.*

Runa sat up with a grin.

HOMESICK

BY ALEIFIR THE BARD

Lead me to the fields of light,
where stars glimmer in pools
and caress the lea-leaves.
Heal me there of the blight
that makes all men into fools
and drives us to the lea-leaves
for solace.
Oh, take me back, before I die,
to the land where soft hills lie
beneath the stars, robed in white.
Oh, take me back to my heart's delight.

Read more *Callenlas Chronicles* from Ref Light:

Reformation Lightning

Kids fiction from a biblical worldview

We create thrilling stories that point to the greatest gospel story, giving truth a clear avenue into kids' hearts and imaginations.

Reformation Lightning is an imprint of 10Publishing and its titles are available through

10ofthose.com